NORMAN
PRICE

BELLA
LASAGNE

JAMES

SARAH

TITLES AVAILABLE IN BUZZ BOOKS

THOMAS THE TANK ENGINE

FIREMAN SAM

TUGS

BUGS BUNNY

BARNEY

MICRO MACHINES

GREMLINS

First published 1990 by Buzz Books,
an imprint of the Octopus Publishing Group,
Michelin House, 81 Fulham Road, London, SW3 6RB.

LONDON MELBOURNE AUCKLAND

Fireman Sam © 1985 Prism Art & Design Ltd.

Text © 1990 William Heinemann Ltd.

Illustrations © 1990 William Heinemann Ltd.
Story by Caroline Hill-Trevor
Illustrations by CLIC!
Based on the animation series produced by Bumper Films for
S4C/Channel 4 Wales and Prism Art & Design Ltd.
Original idea by Dave Gingell and Dave Jones, assisted by
Mike Young. Characters created by Rob Lee.

ISBN 1 85591 031 4

Printed and bound in the UK by BPCC Paulton Books Ltd.

A SURPRISE
FOR SARAH

Story by Caroline Hill-Trevor
Illustrations by CLIC!

Fireman Sam was on his way down to the
fire station when he bumped into Sarah,
James and Norman. "Mornin', you three,"
he said, "off somewhere nice?"

"Oh hello, Uncle Sam," replied James.
"We're going up to Pandy Farm to play."
"It's a beautiful day, isn't it? Enjoy
yourselves." And he went off to work.

Sarah, James and Norman ran off up the lane to Pandy Farm. "I've got an idea," said Norman, when they got there.

"Let's play firemen; you're Fireman Sam, James, I'll be Elvis, and we'll rescue Sarah!"

"But I don't want to be rescued," cried Sarah. "Can't I be a fireman too, and we can all pretend we're rescuing someone?"

"But you're a girl and girls aren't firemen," said James. "Come on, Sarah."

Reluctantly Sarah agreed. "Climb up to the top of the haystack and we'll pretend it's on fire," said Norman.

9

"I'm not sure about this," said Sarah, as she clambered up. "It seems very high. I can touch the roof." When she reached the top bale she caught hold of a beam and sat

10

down on it, swinging her legs in the air.

"Ready," she shouted, looking for the
two boys, "you can start rescuing me now."

James and Norman had disappeared.

"J-a-m-e-s! N-o-r-m-a-n!" Sarah shouted, but there was still no sign of them. "Never mind. I'll just sit here and wait. They're bound to come back."

Sarah waited and waited but the boys didn't come back. "I'm bored with this," she thought, "I might be missing something. I'll get down and go and find them."

But when Sarah looked down, the top bale had slipped down the stack and the next one was too far to jump to. She was stuck. "Now what am I going to do?" she thought, beginning to feel scared. "What if James and Norman don't come back?"

"Help! H-E-L-P!" she shouted at the top of her voice.

"I didn't know Sarah was such a good actress," Norman whispered to James as they put their heads round the barn door. "Anyone would think she was really stuck up there!"

14

"Don't worry, Sarah, Fireman Sam's here now," said James putting on a deep voice, "and I've got Elvis to help me. We'll get the ladder from outside and have you out of here in a jiffy."

Sarah was delighted. "Thank goodness you're here, Uncle Sam. James and Norman wanted to pretend to be firemen and rescue me so I climbed all the way up here. Now I'm really stuck and they've disappeared!"

James and Norman looked at each other. "Oh dear," said James, "I think we need a proper ladder, not a pretend one. You'd better go and call the fire brigade, Norman, while I stay here with Sarah."

"Hello, Sarah," laughed James, "sorry we were so long. Norman wanted to go and see the new foal. Are you all right?"

Sarah grinned. "Oh yes, I'm all right, now Fireman Sam's here, that is. He and

Elvis have just gone to fetch the ladder from
Jupiter and then they're going to rescue me
properly! Don't look so worried, James. You
know we can trust Uncle Sam. Where's
Norman, by the way?''

"I . . . I'm not sure," stuttered James, with his fingers crossed behind his back. "He should be here soon." Norman came racing into the barn. "Don't worry, I've called the

fire brigade. Fireman Sam's already out on
a call but they're sending over the rescue
tender from Newtown. Just hang on a little
longer, Sarah."

"What are you talking about, Norman?" asked Sarah, looking puzzled. "Of course Fireman Sam's out on a call – he's here. He's just gone to get his ladder."

22

"Well actually, Sarah," said James, looking embarrassed, "Fireman Sam isn't here. You must have heard Norman and I pretending."

Sarah burst into tears. "I'm going to be stuck up here all night and it's all your fault. Who says girls can't be firemen? They couldn't be any worse than you two, going off and leaving me like that."

"Who says girls can't be firefighters?" said a voice from outside the barn.

"Firefighter Morris from the Newtown
brigade to your rescue." And in walked
Penny Morris carrying her ladder.

James and Norman couldn't believe their eyes.

"Stop crying now. I'll soon have you down," said Penny, as she stretched out her ladder and put it up against the haystack until it reached the beam.

26

"Hold on, Sarah, I'll come up and
get you." Penny climbed up the ladder.

"What's going on here, James?" said
Fireman Sam, coming into the barn.

"What's Sarah doing up on that beam?"

27

"Oh Uncle Sam, we were pretending to rescue Sarah and she got stuck."

"Well don't worry, she's in safe hands," said Fireman Sam. "Firefighter Morris is a credit to the force."

"There you are, Sarah," said Penny, setting Sarah down safely on the barn floor.

"I bet that was your first firefighter's lift!"

"Thanks, Penny," grinned Sarah. And then she turned to James and Norman, "You weren't pretending to rescue me at all. Next time we play firefighters, bags I be Penny Morris, and I'll rescue you two single-handed!"

FIREMAN SAM

STATION OFFICER
STEELE

TREVOR EVANS

ELVIS
CRIDLINGTON

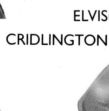

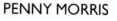

PENNY MORRIS